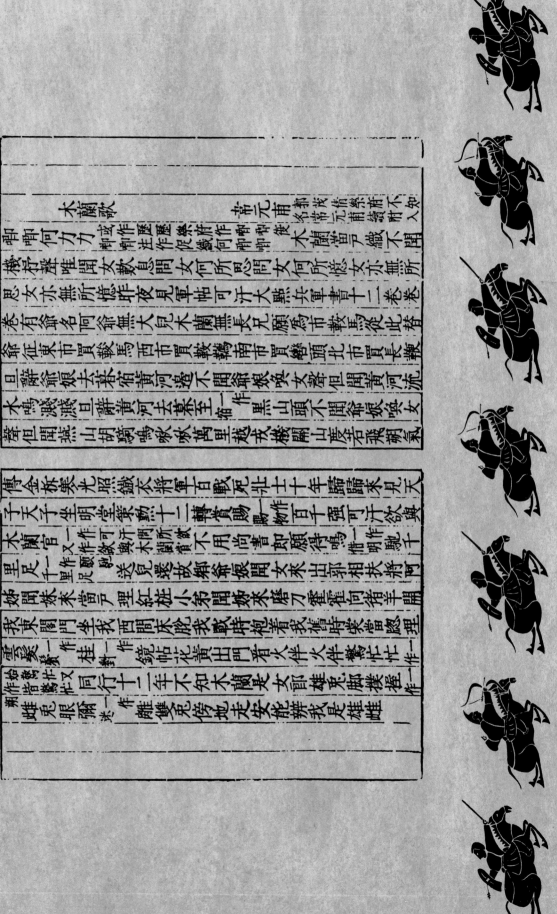

木蘭歌

唧唧復唧唧，木蘭當戶織。不聞機杼聲，惟聞女歎息。
問女何所思，問女何所憶。女亦無所思，女亦無所憶。
昨夜見軍帖，可汗大點兵，軍書十二卷，卷卷有爺名。
阿爺無大兒，木蘭無長兄，願為市鞍馬，從此替爺征。

東市買駿馬，西市買鞍韉，南市買轡頭，北市買長鞭。
旦辭爺娘去，暮宿黃河邊，不聞爺娘喚女聲，但聞黃河流水鳴濺濺。
旦辭黃河去，暮至黑山頭，不聞爺娘喚女聲，但聞燕山胡騎鳴啾啾。

萬里赴戎機，關山度若飛。朔氣傳金柝，寒光照鐵衣。
將軍百戰死，壯士十年歸。

歸來見天子，天子坐明堂。策勳十二轉，賞賜百千強。
可汗問所欲，木蘭不用尚書郎，願馳千里足，送兒還故鄉。

爺娘聞女來，出郭相扶將；阿姊聞妹來，當戶理紅妝；小弟聞姊來，磨刀霍霍向豬羊。
開我東閣門，坐我西閣床，脫我戰時袍，著我舊時裳，當窗理雲鬢，對鏡帖花黃。
出門看火伴，火伴皆驚忙：同行十二年，不知木蘭是女郎。

雄兔腳撲朔，雌兔眼迷離；雙兔傍地走，安能辨我是雄雌。

To all women, young and old

THE SONG OF MULAN

JEANNE M. LEE

Front Street
Arden, North Carolina

Click, click. Click, click.
Mu Lan is at her loom.
We no longer hear her weave.
Now we only hear her sigh.
Why does Mu Lan sigh?
Why is Mu Lan sad?

唧唧復唧唧，木蘭當戶織，不聞機杼聲，
惟聞女歎息。問女何所思，問女何所憶。

"I do not sigh.
I am not sad.
Last night I heard the call to arms:
The Emperor is raising an army.
Twelve times I heard the call to arms,
And each time, my father's name."

女亦無所思，女亦無所憶。昨夜見軍帖，
可汗大點兵，軍書十二卷，卷卷有爺名。

Father has no elder son.
Mu Lan has no older brother.
"I wish I were on horseback.
I would ride in Father's place."

阿爺無大兒，木蘭無長兄，
願為市鞍馬，從此替爺征。

East to buy a horse.
West to buy a saddle.
South to buy a harness.
North to buy a whip.

東市買駿馬，
西市買鞍韉，
南市買轡頭，
北市買長鞭。

"At dawn I leave my home.
That night I sleep by the Yellow River.
I hear my father's voice no more,
Only the rush of the river.

旦辭爺孃去，暮宿黃河邊。
不聞爺孃喚女聲，
但聞黃河流水鳴濺濺。

"At dawn I leave the Yellow River.
That night I reach the black hills.
I hear my mother's voice no more,
Only the enemy's horses neighing.

旦辭黃河去，暮宿黑山頭。
不聞爺孃喚女聲，但聞燕山胡騎聲啾啾。

"Ten thousand miles to the border.
I cross high mountains as if on wings.
War drums ring in the brittle air.
The cold moon shines on steel."

萬里赴戎機，
關山度若飛。
朔氣傳金柝，
寒光照鐵衣。

Great generals of a hundred battles perish.
But foot soldiers go on ten long years.

将軍百戰死，
壯士十年歸。

"I live to greet the Son of Heaven,
The Son of Heaven in the Imperial Court.
He gives me twelve medals of honor
And a thousand strings of gold."

歸來見天子，天子坐明堂。
策勳十二轉，賞賜百千強。

What do you wish? asks the Son of Heaven.
"I do not want honors or gold,
  But strong camels to carry me
  Many miles, back to my village."

可汗問所欲，木蘭不願尚書郎。
願借明駝千里足，送兒還故鄉。

Father! Mother! Hear your daughter return.
Come, hold on to each other.
Elder Sister! Hear Younger Sister return.
Dress to welcome her home.
Younger Brother! Hear Second Sister return.
Sharpen a knife to slaughter a pig and a lamb.

爺孃聞女來，出郭相扶將，
阿姊聞妹來，當戶理紅妝，小弟聞姊來，
磨刀霍霍向豬羊。

"I enter the east gate,
Then sit on the bed in my room.
First I take off my armor,
Then put on an old dress.
I comb my hair at the window
And pin on a yellow flower.

開我東閣門，
坐我西閣牀，
脫我戰時袍，
著我舊時裳；
當窗理雲鬢，
對鏡貼花黃。

"I go to meet my comrades.
Together for twelve years,
My comrades will be startled.
They do not know I am a woman."

出門看火伴，火伴皆驚惶：
同行十二年，不知木蘭是女郎！

A male rabbit is fast and agile,
A female rabbit has bright eyes.
When the two rabbits run together,
No one can tell which is male, which is female.

雄兔腳撲朔，雌兔眼迷離；
兩兔傍地走，安能辨我是雌雄？

It is believed that this Chinese folk poem originated during the Northern
and Southern Dynasties, A.D. 420 – A.D. 589. It was recorded in court
anthologies as early as the Tang Dynasty. Versions from the Sung and Ming
Dynasties are reproduced here on the endpapers. The verses of the poem
are still taught to children in China today and are sung in Chinese opera in
different dialects.

Copyright © 1995 by Jeanne M. Lee
All rights reserved
Library of Congress Cataloging-in-Publication Data
Mu-lan shih. English
   The Song of Mu Lan / Jeanne M. Lee.
      p.   cm.
   Translation of Mu-lan shih; a folk song about a girl
   called Mu-lan who joined the army to substitute for her father;
   written in Pei ch'ao
      ISBN 1- 886910-00-6 (alk. paper)
      1. Hua, Mu-lan (Legendary character) — Juvenile poetry. I. Lee, Jeanne M.
   PL2668.M83E13 1995
   895.1'142 — dc20
                                        95-9594
Printed in Hong Kong by Blaze I. P. I.
Designed by Susan M. Sherman
First edition

I wish to thank my husband, Patrick, for his infinite patience,
Stephen Roxburgh for his vision, and the Harvard Yenching Library for research done there.

木蘭詩

促織何唧唧，木蘭當戶織。不聞機杼聲，唯聞女歎息。問女何所思，問女何所憶。女亦無所思，女亦無所憶。昨夜見軍帖，可汗大點兵，軍書十二卷，卷卷有耶名。（耶以耶切今作爺俗呼父為爺）阿耶無大兒，木蘭無長兄，願為市鞍馬，從此替耶征。東市買駿馬，西市買鞍韉，南市買轡頭，北市買長鞭。旦辭耶孃去，暮宿黃河邊。不聞耶孃喚女聲，但聞黃河流水鳴濺濺。旦辭黃河去，暮宿黑山頭，不聞耶孃喚女聲，但聞燕山胡騎聲啾啾。萬里赴戎機，關山度若飛。朔氣傳金柝，寒光照鐵衣。將軍百戰死，壯士十年歸。歸來見天子，天子坐明堂。策勳十二轉，賞賜（賜一作物）百千強。可汗問所欲，木蘭不用尚書郎，願馳千里足，送兒還故鄉。耶孃聞女來，出郭相扶將。阿姊聞妹來，當戶理紅妝，小弟聞姊來，磨刀霍霍向豬羊。開我東閣門，坐我西閣床。脫我戰時袍，著我舊時裳。當窗理雲鬢，挂鏡帖花黃。出門看火伴，火伴皆驚忙。同行十二年，不知木蘭是女郎。雄兔腳撲朔，雌兔眼彌離，兩兔傍地走，安能辨我是雄雌。（詩誰知烏之雌雄）